Totally Twins

Tropical Trouble

The Fabulous Diary
of Persephone Pinchgut

Sweet Cherry
Publishing

Author
Aleesah Darlison

Illustrator
Serena Geddes

Published by Sweet Cherry Publishing Limited
Unit E, Vulcan Business Complex
Vulcan Road
Leicester, LE5 3EB
United Kingdom

www.sweetcherrypublishing.com

First published in the UK in 2016
ISBN: 978-1-78226-297-8

Published by Sweet Cherry Publishing in 2016

First published in Australia in 2010 by
New Frontier Publishing

Text copyright © 2010 Aleesah Darlison
Illustrations copyright © 2010 Serena Geddes

Tropical Trouble: The Fabulous Diary of Persephone Pinchgut

Series: Darlison, Aleesah. Totally twins.
Target Audience: For primary school age.
Other Authors/Contributors:
Geddes, Serena.

Designed by Nicholas Pike

Printed and bound in India by Thomson Press India Ltd.

To my family.
Aleesah Darlison

For my niece Nyah who has been the
biggest TT fan from the very beginning.
Serena Geddes

Monday 19 April. 1:15 pm.
On my first ever plane flight.

Ah, I love the smell of blank paper in the afternoon! This is my third fabulous diary and it's totally brand new. I started keeping a diary a few months back so I could have something for myself.

I have an identical twin sister, Portia, who is only two minutes older than me - although she thinks she's so much cooler and more mature. She and I usually share EVERYTHING. Sometimes we even get mistaken for each other because we look so similar.

But I got this idea that keeping a diary would be one thing I could do on my own. I love my diary because it's where I write my innermost secret thoughts, dreams and hopes. It's also where I record the fun things that happen to me.

Anyhow, if you're reading this - which you most definitely should be, as long as you're not Portia - then you're reading my first exciting entry. I have a whole book to fill and I intend to make this diary as fabulously unforgettable as the last two. But this new diary isn't just any diary.

It's a TRAVEL diary.

Why, you ask?

Because I'm travelling, of course!

For the first time ever I'm flying on a plane: overseas. Literally, I'm flying over the ocean right now. How cool is that? I even have a passport, although you don't want to see the photo of me in it because when I had it taken I wasn't allowed to smile. Apparently, it's the law for passport photos. A rule against smiling seems wrong to me.

Anyhow, before I get on my 'soapbox', as Gran would say, I'd better fill you in on what's happening.

A few weeks ago Gran promised to take Portia and me to Fiji for the school holidays. Thankfully she kept her promise so now we're winging our way towards two whole weeks in PARADISE.

We're staying at a posh hotel. It's called

the Coconut Cove Resort. Pure bliss!

Gran is a travel writer so she goes on loads of holidays then writes reviews and reports about them, which then get published in newspapers and books. She's famous in a way, although people usually don't recognise her face, only her name, which is Lucille Tench. You may have heard of her.

Gran isn't like other grandmothers who like lavender and lace and cats. She likes bungy jumping and skydiving and jetskiing instead. She's quite adventurous.

Although Gran goes on many holidays for her job, this is the first time she has ever taken Portia and me with her. She says we're now at an 'easy' age so apparently we're a breeze to look after.

I'm not sure Portia is at an easy age, or

ever will be. She's high maintenance if you ask me, but I wasn't going to disagree with Gran. Not if it cost me two weeks in Fiji.

So, we're flying over the beautiful blue ocean and I couldn't be happier: except for one minor detail.

We have had to bring our totally annoying seven-year-old next-door neighbour, Dillon Pickleton, aka Dill Pickle, with us.

Oh no, you say!

Oh yes, I say.

This could be a crushing blow to the

enjoyment of our holiday, but I'm trying not to let it get to me. Even though I'm sitting beside Dill right now and he's kicking the seat in front of him in a most annoying way. If it wasn't for the fact that the person sitting in the seat in front of him is Portia, I would tell him to stop kicking it.

I think I will let Portia deal with this one. At the moment, she's giving him the evil eye as she peers through the seats. Dill hasn't noticed, but it's only a matter of time before Portia explodes. Luckily the flight to Fiji is only four hours. I don't know how much of sitting beside Dill in a confined space anyone can handle.

Now he needs to go to the toilet and is clambering over me into the aisle. Gran told me to take him so he doesn't get lost or frightened.

'It's only up the end of the aisle,' I said.

She wasn't buying it.

'It's his first time on a plane and he's only seven. Go with him.'

I wanted to argue that it was my first time on a plane, too, but I decided it would be quicker if I just took him.

Back soon. I still have heaps to tell you.

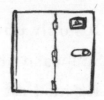

That took longer than it should have.

First, Dill and I couldn't work out how to open the folding toilet door. It took us ages and Dill was absolutely busting to go. I don't know why little kids hold on until the last moment. It often leads to accidents!

We were rattling the door and banging it and kicking it until finally one of the air hostesses came to sort us out. She was pretty with perfectly white teeth and long, red fingernails and her hair slicked back into a smooth bun.

She smiled and pointed to the red sign above the door that said

'OCCUPIED'.

She explained that meant someone was in there. Then she pointed to another toilet behind us and said it was vacant and we could use it. Of course, that door opened easily and Dill slipped inside.

Because he took for-absolutely-ever, I was left standing in the aisle and the man who had been in the toilet while we were banging on the door finally came out. He looked grumpy, and when he spotted me I went bright red like I was guilty or something, which I guess I was. The guy, who looked a bit like a rock star, wore black jeans, a black shirt and had long, red hair and tattoos, grumbled and shook his head as he said, 'Typical kid.'

Luckily, I got distracted when I saw inside the toilet as the man walked away, otherwise I might have 'developed a complex', as Gran would say. I decided to have a look. Dill was taking forever, so what could it hurt?

I locked myself in and checked out every tiny compartment. Then I pressed the toilet button. I squealed when it made a deafening WHOOSHING noise because I thought I'd done something wrong and that I might get sucked down the tube.

As I burst out of my toilet, Dill burst out of his. He was as white as a ghost and his eyes w filled with big blobs of tears

SWOOOSH

'What's wrong?' I asked.

'The toilet made the loudest noise. I thought I was going to be sucked down it or something,' he said.

'Don't be silly. What a typical kid thing to say!'

Dill, who still looked frightened, said, 'Perse-Portia, can you hold my hand? Just until we get back to our seats?'

Dill often calls Portia and me 'Perse-Portia' because he can't tell us apart. Not that he's the only one.

Rolling my eyes and sighing, I took Dill's hand and led him back to our seats.

Now here I am again, writing furiously.

Once we reach the resort I will be 'making myself scarce', as Gran would say, so Dill can't follow me. I refuse to babysit him the entire holiday, although I'm sure that's what Mum would want me to do.

Actually, the only reason Dill has come with us is because of Mum. She thought she was doing something kind, you know the 'good Samaritan' thing, by suggesting to Mr and Mrs Pickleton that they send Dill to Fiji for two weeks. She said they needed a break.

Mr Pickleton is a real-life hero because he's a fireman. He works shifts, so sometimes he has to go to work in the middle of the night!

Mum thinks this isn't good for the health of Mr and Mrs Pickleton's relationship (whatever that means), so she offered to send Dill with us.

For some reason, Mr and Mrs P jumped at the chance for ALONE TIME, so we're stuck with Dill and I bet they are having a wonderful break.

Hey, the meal tray has arrived. Must eat. I'll write later.

Monday 19 April. 3:20 pm.
Continued.

CONTENTS OF THE SNACK TRAY

1. 1 bag of peanuts (average)

2. 1 teeny-tiny cup of orange juice (not bad)

3. 1 choc-chip cookie (devoured in seconds)

Before I go any further I should fill you in on my family, just in case you haven't already read my two other fabulous diaries. Which, you should, if you want to learn all about the terrific things I get up to and have some awesome laughs at the same time.

MY TWIN SISTER, PORTIA

Like I said, Portia and I are IDENTICAL twins. We're in Year Five at Heartfield Heights Primary School. We're ten: very, very nearly eleven. We live with our mum, Skye, who is into weird and unusual things. When she was pregnant with Portia and me she was into Greek mythology and Shakespeare. That's why she named me after the Goddess of the Underworld and Portia after the heroine in the play, *The Merchant of Venice*, written by that old bearded guy, Shakespeare.

Unlike me, Portia is outgoing and confident. Take her anywhere and she thrives. She's like a weed in that respect. Portia is sometimes what I call a SHOW-OFF. She loves ballet and singing and fashion. She can be bossy and messy, which is annoying because we share a room.

Still, I love her just the same. (Don't tell her I said that or I'll never hear the end of it.)

Oh and so you know, Portia and I have the

same honey-blonde hair, the same crystal-green 'cat's eyes', as Mum calls them, and the same pointy elbows and skinny fingers. The only difference is, I have a teardrop-shaped mole on my left cheek and Portia doesn't. I call it a BEAUTY SPOT. Portia calls it a smudge.

MY MUM

Just like my gran isn't like other grans, my mum isn't like other mums. She's totally organic and alternative. She teaches yoga classes and laughter therapy workshops, usually in our living room. Needless to say, my laughter therapy-teaching mother was not impressed with the 'no smile' rule on the passport photos either.

Despite the weirdness of Mum's jobs,

she's actually very good at them and people love her. Her clients are always 'ommming' and 'ahhhhing' or laughing uncontrollably in our house. It's a little unusual, but good for a giggle. When Mum's clients come around, Portia and I listen from our room.

We usually barricade ourselves in with a supply of chocolate-chip cookies, which we buy with our pocket money and smuggle into the house. Mum's organic outlook on life means she isn't keen on chocolaty or sugary things.

Mum's boyfriend is her college art

teacher, Mr Divine. He's nice, and quite handsome for an elderly-type guy of thirty-something.

MY DAD

My dad's name is Pickford. You may have guessed he doesn't live with us. He moved to England a few years ago and remarried. His new wife is Eleanor Elizabeth Krankston. Her initials are E.E.K. so Portia and I call her EEK! (Tee-hee.)

We don't get to see Dad much because he lives so far away. He phones or texts occasionally, but that's it. I'm trying not to let it get to me, but I do wonder what he will do for our birthday, which is coming up in a month or so. I wish he would come home for it!

MY GRAN

Gran is totally cool. Portia and I both adore her. She does, however, have a habit of buying Portia and me the exact same thing for our birthdays and Christmas. Right down to the same style and colour. She loves showing her twin grandchildren off - always has - and makes sure everyone knows we're twins.

As if you could miss it!

AND FINALLY, ME!

To mix things up, I'm including a list here of the TOP TEN things you need to know about me. Here goes:

1. My full name is Persephone River Pinchgut. Portia's middle name is Flame, BTW.

2. My favourite colour is purple.

3. My favourite foods are chocolate, sushi and chocolate cake.

4. My least favourite food is asparagus. Yuck!

5. I'm into Egyptian archaeology, swimming, reading and collecting stationery. Gel pens are the best.

6. I always wear my hair in a ponytail with four clips on either side so no hair can escape.

7. I would love to go to England one day. I would be able to visit Dad and see his new chocolate shop (which Mum doesn't approve of),

8. My two best friends are Caitlin and Jolie. Pity they couldn't come with us to Fiji, instead of Dill!

9. I am rather shy. I'll let you in on a little secret here. I am so nervous about meeting new kids on this holiday. I hope they like me.

10. And here is another secret: I have a terrible phobia of sharks. I hope I don't meet any in Fiji.

Monday 19 April. 6:15 pm.
Fiji airport.

The Pinchguts have landed!

Normally this would be cause for celebration, having made it through a plane flight, survived the turbulence and rough landing and the million or so questions Dill asked me while we were in the air.

However - and it's a big HOWEVER - our luggage has been lost! Well, Portia's and my luggage, anyhow. Gran and Dill have theirs.

Don't ask me how they lost it. I'm still in shock. So is Gran. She said that after all the flights she's been on she's never had any luggage lost.

This is not a good start to the holiday. My bliss has gone amiss...

While the airline staff are running around like 'chooks with their heads cut off', as Gran would say, and being extremely apologetic, it doesn't change the fact that our suitcases are missing.

We put name tags all over them so hopefully they will turn up. It's not like you could miss the hot-pink suitcase Portia insisted on buying or the mulberry-purple one I bought. Luckily I had my diary with me on the plane. All Portia cared about was her lip gloss, which thankfully she had on her. She just can't do without it.

Gran has promised to buy us new clothes once we get to the resort. Portia is excited about this, but I'm wondering what sort of clothes they will have. Will it all be bright floral prints or will there actually be some nice clothes?

'I could do with a new sarong,' Portia said, when she heard about our lost luggage. Not that she's had a sarong before. I think she's trying to be clever and putting her order in with Gran now so when we reach the resort it's all systems go with the sarong. And whatever else she decides to buy.

When I complained that I liked my old clothes, Portia said it was a blessing in disguise and that it would give me a chance to buy something nice: like I didn't already have nice clothes.

Well, for her information, I think my clothes are nice. Portia the Fashion Princess obviously thinks otherwise.

Monday 19 April. 7.25 pm.
On the bus. Window seat.

Portia is snoring beside me, completely worn out from our early start and the flight. I borrowed Gran's camera to take a snap of her. It's one of those old instant Polaroids (which I love).

This is what Portia looks like when she's sleeping.

Not a pretty sight.

Now I have something on Portia next time she hassles me – which she often does because she says that's her job as my older sister. Although she's only two minutes older than me, she takes her job super seriously.

It's getting dark, and it's hard to see out the window. From what I have seen, though, there are lots of palm trees, lots of barely-clothed children and lots of water.

Almost there!

Gran is checking us in, and I'm checking out the hotel. It's huge, BTW. They use golf buggies to get around the place. The grass is neatly trimmed, there are walkways and buggy paths everywhere and the gardens are lush and divine. Even in the dark, I can see it all because there are lanterns everywhere outside. It gives the resort a warmth or 'ambience', as Gran called it.

Inside the hotel lobby, huge fans rotate on the ceiling. Marble floors, timber furniture and massive arrangements of orchids and other gorgeous smelling flowers are everywhere, not to mention the totally comfy leather lounges. I'm in heaven! Like I said, two weeks in paradise.

Monday 19 April. 8:48 pm.
Hotel suite. Top bunk.

Although our hotel suite is lovely and has a large dining/living room with two bedrooms, we have just discovered there is no hot water in the bathroom. Apparently, Fiji is so hot they don't need hot water. Two weeks of cold showers. Hmmm.

Portia is irate.

'I hope you're going to mark them down in your review for not having hot water,' she told Gran.

Gran sighed. 'Portia, darling, loads of these places don't have hot water. Trust me, you won't need it. It won't affect your holiday whatsoever.'

'Of course it will,' Portia insisted. 'How am I going to get my shampoo to lather in cold water?'

I'M FREEZING!

She has a point, but I don't think it's worth huffing about.

BTW, Portia and I are sharing a bunk bed. I'm on the top bunk. Yay!

Dill has the trundle bed that pulls out from under Portia's bed. So, we're all in one bedroom together. There's nothing like 'economising', as Gran would say. She has a bedroom to herself, and it has a view. I wonder if I can get her to swap.

As Portia and I only have one set of clothes each (the ones we wore all day), Gran is letting us wear her shirts as pyjamas. I must say, Gran has weird taste in shirts. The one I'm wearing has a crazy cockatoo bird print on it. Portia's shirt has every colour of the rainbow on it. It looks like one of Mum's abstract paintings.

I hope these shirts don't give me nightmares.

So much for a holiday sleep-in. Dill Pickle is up far too bright and far too early this morning, bouncing around the room and trying to get us up too. I've resisted him until now, but his nagging is never-ending, so I guess I'll have to give in and get up.

Tuesday 20 April. 7:49 am.
Tall Ships Dining Room.

I have never in all my life seen so much food! According to Gran, this buffet eating style, where tables and tables of food are set out for people to gorge themselves on, is how most resorts operate.

I seriously do not know where to start. Here is a list of some of the food on offer:

1. Fruit
2. Muesli
3. Cereal
4. Bacon
5. Sausages
6. Eggs (boiled, fried, scrambled, poached)
7. Pancakes with maple syrup
8. Ice-cream

Ice-cream for breakfast? Mum would totally not approve of this.

Sorry, I have to go because I must eat. Besides, Portia is sending me a SECRET SIGNAL of annoyance to make me put away my diary.

TTFN (Ta Ta For Now).

True to her word, Gran took us to the resort boutique to buy new clothes. My fears about floral prints were well-founded. Very few clothes didn't have 'I love Fiji' printed on them or weren't in colours so bold they nearly knocked your eyes out. I bought a few outfits. Portia bought heaps, but she reasoned with Gran that if worse came to worse I could wear her clothes too. Gran is such a pushover she basically let Portia buy whatever she wanted. Portia even bought TWO sarongs and they are both exactly the same. Can you believe it? She said she needed two so she could wear one while the other was being washed.

There was almost a major hitch with our

swimsuits. They had a limited range in our size and we nearly had to get the same pair! Gran was excited and said it meant she could dress us like twins, which we haven't let her do in ages.

Portia said wearing the same swimmers was a fashion faux pas (i.e. DISASTER) waiting to happen and for once I agreed with her. Wearing matching clothes when you have matching faces (and matching everything else) is so baby-twinsy. We stopped doing that a long time ago, practically the day we were born.

What would people think if we turned up at the pool dressed exactly the same? It's not like you can avoid the pools in this place. There are seven of them dotted throughout the resort. I read it in the brochure.

We scrounged around the racks and, thankfully, found two different sets of swimmers, much to Gran's disappointment.

Sadly, I think Portia got the better pair of swimmers. Hers is a pink bikini with tiny white polka dots. Mine is a navy-blue and brown one-piece swimsuit that looks like something Gran would wear.

Still, it fits, so I shouldn't complain, even though Portia said she wouldn't be caught dead in it.

Portia also insisted Gran buy her a swimming cap and goggles.

Gran said, 'Really, Portia, you're not entering the Olympics.'

'But chlorine is toxic,' Portia replied. 'In science I learnt they used it in mustard gas in the war. Imagine what it might do to my hair.'

She twirled a handful of her hair at Gran. 'You don't want this turning green, do you? Look at it! It's glorious.'

This was TOTT (totally over the top), even by Portia's Fashion Princess standards, but Gran fell for it. She let Portia buy a hot-pink swimming cap with 'I love Fiji' printed on it. To protect her eyes from the ravages of chlorine, Portia got hot-pink goggles with daisies on the straps.

As we were walking back to our hotel suite, I whispered to Portia, 'Honestly, you'd think the pool was full of acid the way you carried on in there.'

'You'll be sorry when your hair turns to green straw,' Portia said, waving her swimming cap at me. 'Then you'll be begging me to borrow this.'

'Whatever,' I said. But I couldn't help touching my hair. I don't want it turning green.

I hope Portia is wrong about this.

Okay, so while I'm not totally certain about this Kids' Club thingy, Gran has assured me I will have the time of my life here. This is yet to be proven.

Of course, Portia waltzed in as confident as could be. She strode straight up to two girls sitting at a table reading magazines and started talking to them. Pretty soon they were laughing and having a great time.

There are no other girls my age here, but there are lots of little ones Dill's age and younger. The rest of the kids are boys, which I'm totally not interested in.

Except one.

Maybe.

His name is Ashton Barnett-Bryson and

he's twelve. His parents run the resort and he knows everything that goes on here. When he's not being homeschooled, he helps out in Kids' Club. Apparently, he does tennis coaching and is a great sailor. Not that I've talked to Ashton. I only saw him on the other side of the room, but I overheard kids whispering about him.

I've been busy looking after Dill ever since we got here. He was so shy at first, I had to hold his hand and practically drag him into the room. He wouldn't talk to anyone and didn't want to be left with any kids his age, so I had to do colouring-in and stuff with him. I wonder if I was like him when I was little.

At home he's never shy. Maybe it's because he doesn't have his mum and dad here. I always went on holidays with my parents when I was Dill's age. We used to have loads of fun together. I miss those days.

Anyhow, I promised myself not to think about that. Not while I'm on holiday.

Oops, Dill is standing at the table watching me while I write. I'd better finish. I don't want him to see.

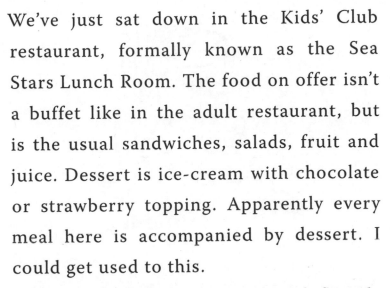

We've just sat down in the Kids' Club restaurant, formally known as the Sea Stars Lunch Room. The food on offer isn't a buffet like in the adult restaurant, but is the usual sandwiches, salads, fruit and juice. Dessert is ice-cream with chocolate or strawberry topping. Apparently every meal here is accompanied by dessert. I could get used to this.

Portia brought her new-found friends over and introduced us. Right now she's rolling her eyes at me and giving me a SECRET SIGNAL of nerdiness, which means she doesn't approve of my diarising at the lunch table.

Luckily, I'm starving, so I will let her SECRET SIGNAL me into putting my diary away for now.

Tuesday 20 April. 2:28 pm.

Raining even more heavily,
which is why I'm still in Kids' Club.

So where was I? Oh, yeah, Portia's new friends.

They're okay, although they are very different to me.

One girl is from Sri Lanka, but lives in France. Her father is a diplomat there. I'm not exactly sure what a diplomat does, but it seems they earn loads of money. She has lovely clothes and shiny jewellery that looks real (not like Portia's plastic stuff), and she speaks like she goes to some posh English school even though she lives in France. She doesn't have any brothers or sisters, but she does have the prettiest hazel eyes and golden skin and a cheeky smile. She's ten like Portia and me, but she acts much older. Her name is Rushani.

The other girl is French, but lives in New Zealand. Weird, huh? Her name is Gigi. She's fully into ballet and horseriding and is a typical girl. She has a strong accent, which is sometimes hard to understand.

I'm terrible with accents so whenever Gigi says something I look at Portia and she interprets for me. Or should I say, she rolls her eyes and then interprets for me.

At lunch, while Portia was collecting her third plate of sandwiches, Rushani said to me, 'Your sister is so confident and friendly. You must really look up to her.'

I didn't realise what she meant so I explained carefully, 'Actually, we're identical twins so she's the same height as me.'

Rushani giggled and said, 'No, I mean you must wish you were more like her. You know, confident.'

I gulped and didn't know where to look and said, 'Sometimes.' Then I scurried away to get another helping of ice-cream with chocolate flavouring.

Still, I can see why Portia has bonded instantly with Rushani and Gigi. She has so much in common with them. They all love ballet and fashion and talking about celebrities and other fluffy, girly stuff. They have been at it practically all day.

Yawn.

Thank goodness I have my faithful diary with me or this day would be a total write-off, what with the dismal weather and the dreary topics of conversation on offer.

When we got back to Kids' Club after

lunch, Portia, Rushani and Gigi started doing ballet twirls and these other pointy-toe moves, which I have no idea what to call or how to do.

I tried several times to tell them there were other things in life besides ballet, but I don't think they believed me because they just kept twirling and giggling.

Boring!

I wanted to see if they liked some of the same things as me so, undeterred, I barged in between their pointed toes and mentioned rather loudly above their giggling that I was into Ancient Egypt and had studied lots about it.

'Did you know that Egyptian mummies that have been dead for over three thousand years still have their fingerprints intact?' I said.

'That's weird,' said Rushani.

'No, it's a true fact.'

'No, it's weird you know that stuff.'

'She knows stacks of weird stuff. Don't

you, Perse?' Portia said as she pointed her toe then did a little jump.

Gigi applauded then did her own pointy-toe-air-jump.

'I sure do,' I said, trying to keep their attention, which wasn't easy because they were so absorbed with their pointy-toe-air-jumping. 'Like when Egyptians mummified someone, they used a special long-handled spoon to scoop the brain out through the dead person's nose. Then they would feed the brain to their animals.'

All three girls shrieked.

'Enough with the horrible facts!' Gigi squealed.

At least that's what I think she said.

Portia shot me a SECRET SIGNAL of severe annoyance. She pulled me aside and said, 'Are you trying to make them think you're strange?'

'No.'

'Then try to be cooler.'

'What, like you? Would that make people like me more?'

Portia rolled her eyes. 'No, just be yourself. Don't try so hard to impress people, at least not by grossing them out. That's never going to work.'

I huffed a bit about that because I couldn't see what was so gross about facts on Ancient Egypt. I like them.

Then Portia offered to teach me some ballet moves, but I didn't think that would win me any popularity contests either. I'm no good at dancing.

'Not everyone likes doing the same things as you, Perfect Portia,' I said. And yes, if I'm completely honest, I was being catty.

'And not everyone likes doing the same things as you, Perse,' Portia replied.

If I'm still being honest, I would have to admit that Portia was trying to be nice, but

I wouldn't let up. It was like I was stuck on a JEALOUSY ROLLERCOASTER that had lost its brakes. Sometimes I feel that way when I sense Portia slipping away from me. She's always good at making friends while I struggle because I'm so different to everyone else. (This is a super-secret confession so please don't tell anyone!)

After that I stormed off and sat in the corner. Dill came over and asked if I wanted to play Mastermind. I looked pretty pathetic sitting by myself so I agreed, but then he got sleepy and had to have a nap. Just like a little kid!

Anyhow, here is a list of five things I'd rather be doing than sitting in Kids' Club right now.

1. Sunbaking by the pool drinking a Coco Colada mocktail
2. Hanging out with Caitlin and Jolie
3. Getting my hair braided
4. Riding on a jet ski
5. Collecting coral

BTW, here is the recipe for a Coco Colada mocktail. I read it on the room service menu.

Coco Colada

- 120 ml pineapple juice
- 60 ml coconut cream
- 1 cup ice
- Orange slice for garnish

When I got a quiet moment with Gran I told her what had happened at Kids' Club. She hugged me and said it was hard meeting new people.

'You're like me,' Gran said. 'I was always so shy. I was never good with words that came out of my mouth, only words I wrote on paper.'

'You're not shy now,' I said.

'No, I grew out of it. You will too. But I'm still good with my writing.' She waved at her laptop. 'And I see you writing in your diary all the time. I like it.'

I told Gran I sometimes wished that Portia and I were more alike. That it might make things easier so we would argue less.

'Portia takes after your mum,' Gran said. 'Skye was always so confident and independent.'

'Was she annoying too?'

Gran laughed. 'Sometimes. I bet you can be annoying, too, when you want.'

Then she playfully tweaked my nose.

That's the thing about Gran. She never takes sides. If Portia and I have an argument she listens and doesn't judge us, she just tries to solve the problem fairly.

'I guess,' I said.

'It's not wrong of Portia to make new friends. It's healthy. It doesn't mean she doesn't love you.'

I thought Gran was getting mushy and I could feel a tight, hot pain in the back of my eyes like I might cry. I knew if I spoke I would definitely start crying, so I just nodded to let Gran know I understood.

It didn't change anything though.

Jealousy hurts.

I'm off to bed. It's been a huge day.

Sleep tight.

We're waiting for everyone to arrive before we head out to the tennis courts. Today is Tennis Comp Day. While I'm happy about this as I love tennis, Portia is complaining. She can't stand tennis or any other ball sports. Give her a pair of dancing shoes or a microphone and there's no stopping her. Give her a bat (or a racquet in this case) and a ball and she struggles.

To get out of playing, Portia is grumbling that it's too hot to play. I know this is a tactic. She's used it before.

While we've been waiting, Portia has been talking to Ashton. When she found out he was from England she got so excited.

'My dad lives in England, Ash!' she

gushed. 'Maybe you know him? His name is Pickford Pinchgut.'

Ashton scratched his head and said, 'Er, no. Sorry. England is pretty big, you know.'

'It's only tiny!' Portia blurted.

'I mean lots of people live there,' Ashton said. 'Like about fifty million.'

'That is a lot,' Portia agreed. 'Anyway, I still want to go there one day. Maybe I could come and visit you?'

You've got to hand it to her, she's persistent.

'Er, sure, if we're living back there then,' Ashton replied politely.

Portia is still hanging out with the others and leaving me with Dill. When I mentioned this to her, she said, 'Perse, can you take care of him? I'll pay you back. Promise.'

When I asked how she could possibly pay me back she wafted on about doing my homework when school goes back, but I know that will never happen.

'What about me?' I said. 'I want to hang out with you.'

I felt pathetic, but it was the truth. I didn't want to be stuck with Dill either.

'Face it, Perse. You've got nothing in common with Rushani and Gigi. You'll just pick an argument or say something silly. You're better off with Dill.'

Grrr.

When we arrived at the tennis courts we had to get picked for teams. Portia and I got picked fairly quickly. So did Rushani and Gigi. They both look coordinated. Portia and I are on the red team while Rushani and Gigi are on the blue team.

Dill was picked last. He's so small and skinny he looks like a five-year-old when really he's seven. Not being picked for things is scarring for a child. I regularly don't get picked for things so I'm practically covered in scars. Still, Dill handled it well. I think he was just happy to finally make it onto a team.

Oops. I've got to go back on court. Portia and I are playing Rushani and Gigi. I have a feeling I will be doing most of the work out there. Wish me luck!

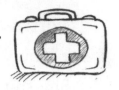

Tennis camp didn't go so well. While Portia and I were playing doubles, I managed to whack her in the eye with the ball. I feel terrible!

I tossed the ball up to serve like I normally do, but this bee flew right in my face and startled me and I whacked the ball funny and Portia turned round at that precise moment and the ball went straight into her eye!

She dropped like a sack of mud and proceeded to roll around on the court, groaning and clutching her face.

'Portia! Are you okay?' I said, as I prised her hands away from her face.

She squinted up at me with a bloodshot eye and tears streaming down her cheeks. 'What did you hit me for?' she yelled. 'You're meant to be on my team!'

'It was an accident, I swear!'

'You did it to get back at me for making new friends, didn't you?'

'Portia, I'd never do that!'

I think she knew it was true. I guess she could see it by the look on my face.

She nodded. 'I believe you. Sorry. It just really hurts.'

By then Rushani and Gigi had arrived and were tut-tutting at Portia's dramatic injury. I'm sure they blamed me.

Portia started complaining that she had sunstroke and needed to be taken to the first aid room to lie down. So Ashton helped Portia up and brought her here. I had to follow after them feeling terribly guilty.

Now Portia is lying on the sick bed ordering me about, asking me to fetch her glasses of water and icepacks and all sorts of things. Whenever she's sick she milks it for all its worth. My guilt at (accidentally) hitting her means I'm letting her get away with it. For now.

When Gran picked us up from Kids' Club she asked Portia if she enjoyed the tennis camp. Portia sat up on the lounge like a corpse rising out of a coffin, plucked the icepack off her eye and said, 'No. All we did was play tennis.' Then she flopped back down on the lounge.

'Well, that is the idea of a tennis camp,' Gran said.

Then Portia just had to add, 'Plus, Perse gave me a black eye.'

Gran and I both inspected Portia's eye and it was nowhere near black. It wasn't even red anymore. Gran told Portia to stop being a drama queen and to get off the lounge so we could go back to our hotel suite to get ready for dinner.

Portia groaned loudly before complaining of sunstroke again.

Gran wasn't at all concerned and told her to 'stop making a scene'.

That's when Dill cut in with one of his bizarre jokes.

'Why did Dillon stare at the apple?' he asked, waving a green apple at Gran, which he had drawn a face on with a black marker.

Gran said she didn't know.

Portia groaned again.

'Because the apple was staring at him,' Dill laughed, terribly pleased with himself.

And if you get that joke you've got a better sense of humour than me.

We've just finished dinner. I swear they had thirty-seven varieties of dessert on offer, all different from last night.

When we walked in, Portia, who seems completely recovered from her black eye and sunstroke, said, 'Check out the seafood! I can't wait to eat those prawns.'

'Are you crazy?' I said. 'What about the dessert bar?'

Portia shook her head. 'Mum would have a breakdown if she saw all this food. She'd say it's a waste.'

Gran smiled. 'What your mother doesn't know won't hurt her, Portia. What happens on holiday stays on holiday.'

We all giggled about that then raced over

to grab our plates.

I think I tried every dessert. Gran didn't mind. She reckons we should 'live a little'. I guess she knows how super-strict Mum is with food at home so she's letting us eat what we want.

Although, I do feel strange in the tummy after all the custard, cream, toffee and chocolate I ate.

Dill wouldn't touch dessert. All he had was a sausage and a slice of bread. Honestly, he could have eaten that back home. Mrs Pickleton isn't what you would call a fabulous cook. She's strictly a meat and three vegies kind of person. Although, she is handy with a sewing machine and has made Portia and me several fancy dress outfits in the past.

When Dill tried his sausage, he said,

'Hmm, this tastes like cheese.'

Portia shook her head at that and went back to eating her prawns.

Then Dill tried his bread (after he sniffed it). 'This tastes like cheese too,' he said.

Gran tried convincing him to eat something else, but he said he wasn't hungry.

I asked him if he was missing his mum and he went red in the face and stared at the tablecloth and mumbled, 'No.'

I'm guessing something isn't right, but he won't spill the beans so I can't force it out of him. Maybe he's homesick.

I miss Mum, too, but don't tell anyone. They might think I'm being a baby.

I felt so sorry for Dill and couldn't stand his mopey face any longer so I offered to take him for a walk, which is why I'm on the beach.

Better go. Dill is shoving shells at me and sprinkling sand down the back of my neck. Boys!

Thursday 22 April. 4:08 pm.
On the beach, again.

I haven't had a chance to write all day because we've been so busy. I've snuck out to be myself and write this so Portia can't see.

When I say we were busy, I don't mean good busy. We were actually in dire peril for a while. Life and death stuff, but now everything is fine.

So, here's the scoop.

The Kids' Club activity today was sailing. We had to go out on the ocean on catamarans. In case you don't know what a catamaran is, it's a boat with a platform that sits on two hulls beneath. It has a sail as well.

I've never been sailing before, but Portia

insisted we go. Ashton gave everyone a few pointers. We learned about steering and tacking and that sort of thing.

We all wore lifejackets, although Portia said yellow didn't suit her colouring. I guess it didn't look great on me either. Still, I wasn't concerned about the lifejackets, but rather falling into the water. Remember point ten on my list, the one about sharks?

But Portia said if I didn't go with her she would go with Rushani and Gigi. I didn't want that to happen. Besides, Dill practically begged us to take him so I had to go. There was no way Portia would have taken him unless I went too.

With Portia's words, 'What could possibly go wrong?' ringing in my ears, I set out with her and Dill.

We sailed out into deep water without any trouble because the wind was blowing super-strong. But no matter how hard we tried, we couldn't get the catamaran back to shore. We tried for hours, but the wind kept taking us further out to sea!

I started to panic. Dill started crying. Portia got stroppy because she couldn't control the stupid catamaran. We were all getting angry with each other. Portia refused to call out for help because she said it would be too embarrassing.

Eventually, I convinced her that calling for help was our only option so we all stood up on the boat, waving our arms in the air and yelling at the top of our lungs.

Of course, Ashton was the one who saved us.

Portia was right. It was embarrassing. He rode a catamaran out with some other boys, jumped on our boat and then sailed us back to shore while the other boys followed. I could hear them laughing all the way. Ashton was very good about it and didn't tease us or make jokes. I think he could tell we were mortified. Because his parents own the resort I suppose he can't exactly make fun of the guests.

Portia hasn't stopped talking about Ashton since the 'catamaran incident'. She's calling him our 'knight in shining armour'. Oh, please!

'I've always wanted a hyphenated name,' she said. 'It sounds so sophisticated, don't you think? If I married Ashton, I'd be Portia Barnett-Bryson. Cool, huh?'

I stared at her like she was mad, even though the thought had crossed my mind too.

Persephone Barnett-Bryson. That sounds cooler. Not that I would ever mention it to anyone. Not that it will ever happen.

I mean, what am I thinking? Who considers marriage at the age of ten? Only girls like Portia would do that.

But sometimes these things are fun to think about.

Friday 23 April. 8:57 am.
Hotel suite.

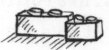

After several days of feeling left out, I've decided that if 'I can't beat 'em, I may as well join 'em', as Gran would say.

I'm going to be more Portia-like. Maybe then the others will like me.

I told Portia I would meet her at Kids' Club as I still had to put my shoes on. Dill was still playing with his Lego and Portia refused to take him so I will take him when I go. Nothing new there.

Before she left, I made sure I saw what Portia was wearing (green sarong, pink T-shirt) and how she had her hair (two plaits, for a change). Then I dressed exactly the same as her and did my hair the same way. I even used some of her lip gloss (don't tell).

I'm sure this will make people like me more.

After all, the Portia thing works for her. Why won't it work for me?

Today has been a total disaster.

Portia absolutely spat it when she saw me walk into Kids' Club wearing her other green sarong and a pink T-shirt and looking exactly like her with plaits and jewellery and everything.

I sat at the table with Portia and Rushani and Gigi, pretending not to notice the fast and furious SECRET SIGNALS Portia was sending me like: 'What do you think you're doing?' 'Have you lost your mind?' 'Why are you ignoring me?'

Instead, I started going through their magazines, cracking the same jokes Portia would have made. And I know she would have made those jokes because I've heard them a thousand times before.

Rushani and Gigi didn't seem to mind at the start, but the day got worse.

I tried doing ballet with them and ended up stepping on their feet. I tried following Portia around and laughing at the other girls' jokes. I even made sure I laughed the same way Portia does with that funny snort-giggle thingy.

Eventually, Portia pulled me aside and asked me what I was doing.

'Having fun,' I told her. 'How about you?'

'Have you gone crazy? You're copying everything I do. It's so baby-twinsy.'

I slumped and stared at the ground. Portia was sick of me being her. So was I. I wanted to be me again.

'I thought being more like you would make people like me,' I explained.

'What made you think that?'

I shrugged. 'Why can't you hang out with me? Those other girls are boring.'

'I'm trying to hang out with everyone, but you make it difficult when you're so annoying.'

'Oh, now I'm annoying. Thanks very much.'

I tugged her jewellery off my arms and angrily pulled my plaits out. 'I don't need this.'

As I turned to storm off, Portia grabbed my arm. 'Perse, I can't help it if people like me. If you gave Rushani and Gigi a chance you'd see they're okay. Just because they like different things to you doesn't mean they're not smart or nice.'

'They're not like Caitlin and Jolie.'

'They shouldn't have to be. That's what makes them interesting.'

Part of me could see what Portia was saying, but another part of me was too grumpy and jealous.

I miss my friends.

I miss Mum.

I'm homesick!

After Kids' Club, Gran came and picked us up and took us to the pool. On Portia's request, Gran bought us some afternoon tea of hot chips and mini-franks. Don't tell Mum. She'd mini-freak out.

Portia is still fuming about me dressing the same as her. I'm still fuming about feeling left out. Dill is still mopey about something he won't talk about, and he's still saying that everything tastes like cheese. Although, he did make up a joke a minute ago.

This is how it goes:

Dill: 'What do you call it when it rains plums?'

Me: 'I have no idea.'

Dill: 'A plumderstorm.'

Me: 'Groan.'

Gran: 'You know, Dillon, you have a very active imagination.'

Dill: 'My teachers tell me that all the time.'

Gran: 'I'm not surprised.'

Portia refuses to go in the pool, BTW. Even with the goggles and swimming cap. She's concerned the pool will fade her new swimmers so she's practically melting away on her banana lounge. She's welcome to fry. I'm going for a swim.

TTFN.

Saturday 24 April. 3:22 pm.
Hotel bedroom. Top bunk.

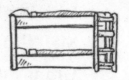

We're having a full day with Gran. Yay! She took us into town to look at the shops. We bought heaps of souvenirs. I bought a shell brooch for Mum and a bandana for Mr Divine. I'm not sure he's the bandana-wearing kind of guy, but it was a good price and it will be light to carry home, which is handy because my suitcase still hasn't turned up. I also bought shell necklaces for Caitlin and Jolie. I bet they love them!

We didn't buy much for ourselves, although Portia insisted on having more hot chips. Goodness knows why.

When I told Gran that Mum says you're just paying for the packaging when you buy junk food, she laughed and said, 'Unless it's fruit, it's got to come in a package. It would be rather difficult carrying ice-cream without the packet, don't you think? Now, Mum's not here so you girls have a good time. Don't worry so much, Perse, and remember, what happens on holiday stays on holiday.'

I think she has a point.

Writing about Mum has made me feel sad. I miss her. I wonder what she's doing. I'm going to ask Gran if I can use her phone to text Mum.

Saturday 24 April. 4:15 pm.

Halfway up a bendy coconut tree.

Why am I halfway up a coconut tree, you ask? This is the only place in the entire resort where Gran's phone can get reception. Totally true!

I tried to send Mum a text five minutes ago, but then I had to climb up here for it to go through. Everywhere else I got an error message.

This is what I sent:

Hey, Mum, how r u? Portia and I r loving Fiji. Gran is heaps of fun. Dill is mopey, but don't tell Mrs P. She would only worry. Luv P&P.

I sent it from both Portia and me, even though Portia doesn't know about the text. It sounds better coming from both of us. We're kind of talking again. It's hard not to when you have to spend every second with each other.

Yay! The phone just beeped. It's a text from Mum.

All good here. Will and I r going out 4 dinner 2nite. Have been doing loads of painting. Very inspired at the mo! Look after Dill. He's only little. Luv Mum xx.

Looks like today is going to be a lazy day. I don't think we will do much, probably relax by the pool with Gran and Dill.

I wonder if Ashton will be around today. Will he notice me?

I know he notices Portia. She's always talking to him or he's always helping her do something like taking her to sick bay with a tennis injury or saving her from getting swept out to sea on a catamaran.

Portia is always so good at making friends, which I guess helps me in one way. Portia being so outgoing usually does make things easier for me. I just follow her lead. She's great to have around like that.

On the downside, because we are twins

we do tend to stand out, which Portia loves, but I hate. I don't like people noticing me. Another downside of Portia's confidence is that she tends to take over. If I don't stand up for myself, she does all the talking for both of us.

Usually this is okay, but I wanted this holiday to be different. I wanted someone to notice me, and it would have been nice if that someone was Ashton. But things don't seem to be working out that way.

I could mention this to Portia, but I'm too embarrassed to admit I like Ashton. And what if Portia really, really likes him? I don't want a boy to come between us. It's not worth it.

Portia has had a run-in with a ball. Again! This time it was a basketball.

Rushani, Gigi, Portia and I were playing basketball down at the courts when Portia tripped and twisted her ankle. And wouldn't you know it, it was right when Ashton showed up.

Anyway, Ashton ran over to help Portia: again.

'Oh, isn't he so sweet?' Gigi said in her French accent, which for once I understood. 'What a gentleman!'

'I think he likes Portia,' Rushani said.

We watched as Ashton helped Portia limp over to his dad's golf buggy.

Inside I was fuming and my stomach was

tense, but I didn't let on. I'm sure Portia didn't mean to fall over on purpose, but it's funny the way things turn out.

'Hey, Perse, do you want a lift too?' Ashton called over to me.

I thought I should go with Portia so I said yes, even though I wanted to stay with Rushani and Gigi and play basketball and get to know them better.

Ashton really is a gentleman. He held my hand and helped me into the golf buggy to squeeze in beside Portia in the back seat so his dad could drive us to the first aid room. I didn't even have a sore ankle or anything.

Portia is back on her feet, with no permanent damage done to her ankle: funny about that! I think she was trying to avoid playing basketball as it wasn't her idea to play in the first place. Today we're back in Kids' Club.

When I asked Gran why we had to go to Kids' Club again, she said it was because she was here on a working holiday, which meant she had to work. She also said that at least Kids' Club was fun, and that Portia, Dill and I could hang out with kids our own age and there weren't any old 'wrinklies' like her cramping our style.

I'll admit she made some good points.

The schedule of activities for this week

has been pinned up on the noticeboard. There are some fantastic things on the list, as well as a few not-so-fantastic things.

Tomorrow we go to Harmony Island. It's a tiny, uninhabited island just off the coast. We can go fishing and snorkelling and have a barbeque and play beach games. It sounds like fun, except for the snorkelling. I wonder if I can get out of that.

There are some other cool activities later in the week. The most worrying activity is Friday night's Disco Dance-Off. We have to dress up using the Kids' Club wardrobe stock and then perform a dance either by ourselves or in groups. They are running dance lessons all week to help us get into the swing of things.

Get it? Swing of things. Ha ha, sometimes I crack myself up.

I have to say the Disco Dance-Off will be my least favourite activity for the week. Naturally, Portia is thrilled about it. So are Rushani and Gigi.

Typical girls.

Monday 26 April. 11:58 pm.

Hotel bedroom.

Top bunk. Writing in secret.

I don't want to go on this boat ride to Harmony Island tomorrow.

Why? Remember point ten on my list: the sharks? I'm afraid of them. Very, very afraid. Like PETRIFIED afraid.

It's one thing to swim in the pool where it's safe. The only real dangers in pools are the suspicious warm spots or stray beach balls. But in the ocean... well... there are sharks in there. I'm worried that if we go snorkelling tomorrow a shark might bite me.

I did some research before we came to Fiji and discovered there are several dangerous sharks in the waters.

DANGEROUS SHARKS

1. Tiger Sharks
2. Oceanic White Tips
3. Bull Sharks

These kinds of sharks are known to eat people!

Around Fiji there are also other fish with teeth, like barracuda and moray eels, but it's the sharks that terrify me.

Not happy.

I can't sleep.

Tuesday 27 April. 7:15 am.
Hotel bedroom.

I have tried to get out of going today by pretending to be sick, but Gran won't have a bar of it. She said I need to get out in the sun and enjoy myself. Besides, she has a deadline for an article for some travel magazine and needs to work. Alone.

So, it's off to the ocean - and possibly a shark-feeding adventure - I go. Gulp.

Tuesday 27 April. 8:32 am.
On a mini-bus, driving to the boat
for our trip to Harmony Island.

My second attempt at getting out of the Harmony Island trip has failed. I tried begging the Kids' Club carers and tour guides to leave me behind, but they insisted that all of us kids had to stay together. Double gulp.

Tuesday 27 April. 8:46 am.
At the harbour jetty. I'm refusing to get on the boat.

My third attempt at getting out of the Harmony Island excursion is currently underway. I have informed the Kids' Club carers and tour guides that there are too many kids to fit on the boat and not enough lifejackets and that they would be better off letting some of us (i.e. me) stay behind.

And no, I don't care that Ash is here and seeing this performance. I still don't want to get on the boat.

The other kids scurried onto the boat like excited schoolchildren (which is what they are, I suppose), pushing and shoving each other. The Fijian guides laughed and told them to slow down. They said we were on 'Fiji time' now.

But I have set up camp on the jetty and am refusing to move. I'm on slower-than-Fiji-time because I'm not going anywhere.

Oh, drat. They've just found where I stashed the lifejackets. Uh-oh, now they are walking towards me with determined strides.

Goodbye cruel world.

On a tiny boat. In the open ocean.

After being frogmarched onto this tiny tin can, I was wedged in between Portia and Dill and warned not to make any more trouble or hide any more lifejackets.

I agreed, under protest. I know my fear of sharks is making me naughty and unbearable, but I can't help it.

We're packed in like sardines on the tiniest motor boat I've ever seen. When I mentioned this to Portia - pointing out the inherent dangers of our situation - she laughed and said it was super safe and we were being well looked after.

'Wow, look at you being the drama queen,' she said. 'Usually that's my job.'

'I thought I'd give you a break today,' I

said. 'You're on holiday after all.'

That's when Portia ducked her head and asked me real quiet and gentle and not at all Portia-like, 'What's wrong, Perse? Why don't you want to go to the island?'

Because she was being so kind and sisterly, I crumbled immediately and told her about my fear of sharks.

'Well, stick with me and you'll be fine,' she said.

Like that's going to solve my problems. The shark will just think we're two meals for the price of one!

Before I could reply I got a strange feeling in my stomach like I wanted to throw up. Then, I did. Thankfully it was over the side.

'I've been poisoned,' I wailed.

The carers just laughed and said I was seasick.

Luckily, the island is now in sight. It's beautiful, green and tiny, with white sand all around it.

Uh-oh, gotta go. I think I've got more throwing up to do.

As soon as I stepped onto the beach my seasickness evaporated. Thank heavens, but how do you explain that?

While the carers set up beach games, we set out exploring. It only took thirty minutes to walk around the entire island. We found heaps of shells. When we got back to the camp it was time to do the treasure hunt.

'What's a Trevor Hunt?' Dill asked me.

I had to set him straight because the poor kid has never been on a treasure hunt before! Totally sad.

Some of the bigger kids were fast and sneaky and pushed the little kids out of the way to get to the treasure. It was only chocolates and lollies so it wasn't like it was a big deal, but to the little kids it was. It's like at parties where there is a piñata (which I don't like because someone always gets hurt) and the lollies go everywhere and the big kids always get the most. There is always one little kid who ends up crying because he didn't get enough lollies - or any at all.

The treasure hunt ended the same way because Dill and a few other little kids scored almost no lollies. But I shared mine with Dill, and Portia, Rushani and Gigi shared theirs with some other girls who were crying.

'You know, Perse-Portia, I wish I had a sister like you,' Dill said.

I laughed. 'You're only saying that because I gave you lollies.'

He looked at me carefully. 'No, I mean it. You're great.'

Then he hugged me and when he pulled away his face was red and he looked embarrassed.

Just then Portia ran up and said we had to go fishing on the boat.

'I don't want to go,' I told her. 'I might get seasick again.'

One of the guides said we would be staying close to the island so there would be no chance of that. So we all clambered back on the boat, me included, but more slowly this time because we're on 'Fiji time'.

The guide drove us out to the reef edge and then cut the motor and dropped anchor. He gave us handlines and some chopped fish for our hooks. Portia, Rushani and Gigi refused to put dead fish heads on their lines so the guides did it for them.

We sat and waited.

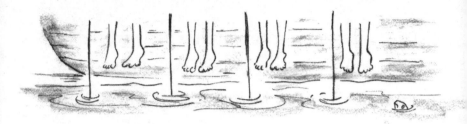

Now we're still waiting, which is why I'm writing: to keep the boredom away. The guide said if we don't catch our lunch, we won't have anything to eat. He laughed when he said it, but we didn't. We're all starving.

Where is the buffet when you need it?

The only person to catch a fish while we were out on the reef was the guide. Even that was so small he had to throw it back in the ocean. But I do have something really funny to tell you.

We were all sitting there getting rather bored and fidgety when the guide hopped up and dived into the water. Portia and I just looked at each other.

'What now?' I asked.

She shrugged. The other kids were shocked, too, and didn't know what to do. Then the guide appeared again, his head bobbing above the green water as it dripped off his black, springy hair.

He climbed back in the boat. But get

this, he had a live octopus with him! Portia, Rushani and Gigi screamed their heads off. It was an amazing sight to see. I thought they were all going to leap into the water to get away from the octopus.

The boys laughed their heads off and yelled, 'Awesome!' as the guide plopped the octopus into the bucket beside his feet and put the lid on. When everyone had settled down, the guide turned the motor on and steered us back to shore.

If I'm not mistaken, I can smell meat cooking on the barbeque. The scent is wafting on the breeze towards us as we near the shore. It looks like we weren't fishing for our lunch after all. They were just kidding. Phew!

I'm completely stuffed. I don't think I've ever eaten a more beautiful meal than the one I just had. Not even at the buffet.

The way the Fijian women cooked our lunch was unbelievable. It was so fresh and delicious that my mouth is still watering just thinking about it.

We had chicken, steak and salad, plus some fresh octopus on the side.

Even though Mum probably wouldn't have approved of the octopus (or the chicken or steak for that matter because she's a vegetarian), I still wish she could

have been here to share this with us. I know she would love the relaxed Fijian lifestyle. It sure makes a change to our rush-rush world back home.

I can't believe I let the others talk me into that! I went snorkelling for the first time ever and it was fantastic. Amazing. Totally wild!

At first, I didn't want to go. I practically begged them not to make me, but Portia said I would regret it if I didn't go.

'This might be your only chance to ever go snorkelling in Fiji. You're crazy not to come along,' she said.

'I'm scared,' I admitted, in a small voice so the others wouldn't hear.

Portia laughed. 'Never mind the sharks. You'll be fine. Besides, it won't be the same without you.'

'Really?' I said. 'Won't you be just as

happy with Rushani and Gigi?'

'No, you ninny, I want my sister to come too.'

That made me feel WONDERFUL. Portia doesn't often say nice things to me.

Another 'contributing factor', as Gran would say, was that if I didn't go, I would have had to stay with Dill and the other little kids. I couldn't stand that, being the only big kid to stay behind. I would rather face the sharks.

I asked Portia if she would at least hold my hand. She sighed and I thought she was going to tell me to stop being a baby, but she just said, 'Sure. If it makes you feel better.'

We put on our flippers and snorkels and swam out in the shallows, over massive stingrays snoozing in the sand. One gave me a fright when it flapped its giant wings as I was passing over it, but somehow I managed to keep swimming and not start  hyperventilating. Luckily Portia was still holding my hand at the time.

I gradually got more confidence and Portia was able to let go, but we still swam side by side. Our hair was flowing in the crystal clear blue water as we gazed at all the fish around us, and we waved to each other whenever we saw something interesting.

While I was swimming I was thinking that Portia was right, this was special. I was glad she made me go because it was something I'd remember forever.

The guide kept swimming, leading us

further and further out across the coral
and away from the island. I didn't know
where we were going to end up and I started
getting worried, but the others were totally
calm so I tried to relax too.

Eventually we made it out to where the
reef dropped away to deep water, like a
cliff dropping away beneath the ocean. I
was super-alert in case there were sharks,
but to my surprise and relief there were
none, just heaps of beautiful fish.

Then we all swam back to shore and

flopped on the sand talking at a million miles an hour and reliving all the fantastic things we'd seen.

That's when Ash said, 'You girls did great. You weren't scared or anything, even though you swam in the most dangerous part of the ocean.'

'Huh?' I gulped.

'You swam to the drop-off. That's where sharks hang out in the deep water waiting for fish to swim by so they can gobble them up.'

That set me off. I thought I might start hyperventilating again, or throwing up, or both. Instead, I fainted.

I woke to find Portia's worried face inches from mine. Dill was beside me, holding my hand and crying.

'What's wrong?' I said. 'I'm not dead.'

He wiped his eyes. 'I know that now.'

'Are you okay, Perse?' Portia asked.

Rushani and Gigi were behind her, looking concerned as well. The guides had picked up a palm frond and were waving it over me to cool me down. Even Ash looked worried as he leaned over me.

I sat up. 'I'm fine. I fainted, that's all.'

'People usually don't faint without a reason,' Portia said.

I tried explaining that I only fainted because of the fright and that I was fine, but Portia wouldn't let me get up.

'I think you've got sunstroke,' she said, 'like I had the other day.'

She insisted on sitting beside me and ordering Dill about, making him fetch me water to drink while the other kids played beach games. She didn't leave my side the whole time and wouldn't let me get up either.

'I think I should get you back to the hotel,' Portia said.

But I vetoed that. I didn't want everyone else having to pack up and go home because of one tiny fainting spell.

I was getting bored, though, so I asked her to pass my diary. I've been scratching away in here ever since. Portia keeps feeling my forehead. Argh, I just had to swat her hand away again.

Ash has checked on me a few times. He called me 'the patient'. Rushani and Gigi have been great too.

Maybe I should faint more often. It sure is one way of getting attention.

Don't tell Portia I'm enjoying it though. She might stop being nice. I like her like this.

Tuesday 27 April. 6:04pm.
Hotel suite. Sunburnt.

I can't believe how sunburnt I got today. My face is bright red and my arms are burning hot. Ouch! Now I have to go to dinner like this. I hope Ash doesn't see me. He will laugh at me for sure.

I'm waiting for Portia to get ready before going to Kids' Club again. We have to practise our dance moves today and I'm dreading it. We have left it to the last minute, of course.

Thankfully, the sunburn has disappeared. Gran has this aloe vera gel that works wonders. Now I can face the world again.

I was thinking I would practise a dance with Dill to cheer him up so he doesn't feel so homesick. Just because he doesn't know any dance moves doesn't mean he can't learn.

I've decided to teach him the macarena. It's standard stuff. They play it at most discos. Even I can dance the macarena, thanks to Caitlin, who taught me last year.

I drew the moves on a piece of paper and showed Dill. It might not be ballet, but it's something. And with my two left feet, it's as complex as it's going to get.

Gran and Portia are relaxing in hammocks between the palm trees and I'm helping Dill build a sand sculpture. He's actually very good. He made a replica of his dog, Camelot.

When I asked him why he was doing Camelot, he said, 'Because I miss her.'

I wonder if he has been missing her all along. I took a photo of him and the sand sculpture with Gran's camera. He was happy about that and said it was almost as good as having Camelot here with him.

I suppose it's different for Dill. I always have Portia around and never get lonely. In fact, I often wish Portia would go away, especially when she's being super Portia-like and annoying!

But Dill has no one because he's an only child.

'Do you think Camelot is missing me?' he asked.

'I bet she is,' I said.

'Maybe one day she'll have puppies,' he said. 'Then I might get more brothers and sisters.'

'Is that how you think of her? Like a sister?'

Dill nodded. 'And a best friend.'

'Do you wish you had a brother or sister?'

'I wish I had a twin, but Mum said she can't help me with that. Maybe when I get home I'll ask Mum for a little brother or sister. Hey, do you want me to make you a sand kitten?'

'Why?' I asked.

'Because you like kittens, don't you?'

'How do you know?'

Dill explained that he remembered ages ago when he was four and went to the shops with Mum and Portia and me that when we went past the pet store I stopped to check out the kittens. According to Dill, I drove Mum mad because she was in a hurry, but I had to make sure I petted them all.

'I forgot about that,' I said. 'Mum and Portia won't let me get a kitten.'

'That's why I gave you the Valentine's Day card,' Dill said. 'You know, the one with the kitten on it.'

I froze. I remembered the card. It had been left on our front porch and was addressed to Portia. I'd assumed it came from a secret admirer, possibly Flynn MacIntosh from our class.

'That was you?' I said. 'Why didn't you sign it?'

Dill shrugged. 'I thought it would be more mysterious if I didn't.'

'You got that right, but why did you write it out to Portia?'

'I got confused,' Dill blushed. 'I'm only seven, you know, and I'm always getting you two mixed up.'

'Tell me about it,' I said, rolling my eyes.

'Plus you play tricks on me.'

It was my turn to blush. 'Yeah. I guess you're right.'

'That's why I sometimes call you Perse-

Portia,' Dill said.

I chewed my lip, feeling awfully guilty.

I'd never talked to Dill like this before. I guess I've never given him a chance. Listening to him made me realise he wasn't so bad after all. Sure, he was annoying and weird sometimes, but he was just a normal kid. Perhaps I was annoying when I was seven too. Or probably it was more likely that Portia had been.

When Dill finished the kitten sand sculpture I took a picture of that too.

I might speak to Mum or Mr Divine about art lessons for Dill. Maybe he could make a new friend there so he wouldn't feel so lonely.

Wednesday 28 April. 9:17 pm.
In the lounge room.
Almost time for bed.

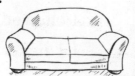

'Are you kidding?'

That's what Portia said when I told her she should be nicer to Dill.

'He behaves for five minutes and you think he's your best friend?'

I tried telling her it wasn't like that, but she wouldn't listen. I tried telling her that she should go easy on him because he's homesick and missing Camelot.

All she said was, 'You've obviously forgotten the water bombing incident of two weeks ago. Also, what about when he dobbed on us for sneaking cookies from his mum's kitchen cupboard? He's a troublemaker.'

'He's just a kid,' I said.

'What about how he calls us Perse-Portia? I know that gets on your nerves.'

'Well, yes...'

'So, case closed. We only have three more days of this holiday and I don't want to spend it hanging out with Dill. Unlike you, I have other friends here, Perse.'

Ouch!

I guess she is back to being not nice. Maybe I should try fainting again.

Thursday 29 April. 4:00 pm.
By the pool.

Gran has finally emerged from our hotel suite where she was putting the finishing touches to her travel book. While Gran was working, Portia, Dill and I had to hang out at Kids' Club again. Luckily we had dance moves to perfect, so that kept us busy.

It's fun being down at the pool though. I've already had a swim. Portia still refuses to get in. She's totally paranoid about the chlorine and is sitting in the shade with Rushani and Gigi reading magazines.

Uh-oh, Ashton just arrived and is waving to me.

TTFN.

Well, that was a disaster. Ashton arrived at the pool and straight away called me Portia. I was too shy to correct him so I didn't say anything. I had to go to the bathroom and when I came back Portia was sitting with him.

He was calling her Perse and she didn't correct him either. When I got back she winked at me like it was some great joke. I had to pretend to be Portia while she pretended to be me.

I guess Ashton hasn't got the hang of telling us apart. I don't know whether this is a good thing. Does he like the real me? Or does he like the Portia version of me? Does he even know there is a difference?

So many questions to be answered!

Why am I even bothering to ask questions about a boy?

Thursday 29 April. 5:32 pm.
Hotel suite.

I ♥ FIJI

Remember the hot-pink swimming cap I told you Portia bought to protect her hair from the ravages of the chlorinated pool?

Well, Portia wore it when she went swimming just now. Yes, she finally went in the pool because Ashton asked her to. How could she resist?

Anyhow, it seems the cap wasn't made with a water-safe dye because most of it has come out. Unfortunately, it has come out all over Portia's hair!

She's in the (cold) shower right now trying to scrub the hot-pink out of it with copious amounts of shampoo. It still hasn't come out though. Not even after seven washes.

You should have heard her scream when she got back to our hotel suite and looked in the mirror. She sounded like she was being attacked. She's going to look a fright at dinner, I can tell you. Teehee.

Thursday 29 April. 7:02 pm.

At the beach. Watching the sun slide over the horizon.

I came down here to take Dill for a walk after dinner. He's getting on Portia's nerves, which are frazzled because of her hot-pink hair. At dinner she tried pretending she had intentionally dyed her hair, but I don't think it washed with the others.

Get it? Washed with the others. Ha ha, sometimes I crack myself up. Again!

Mum sometimes talks about this thing called karma, which means you get back what you give out. Perhaps the hot-pink hair is karma for Portia being mean to me about not having friends here.

Still, I do feel sorry for her. She has got lovely hair: usually.

Teehee.

Friday 30 April. 9:54 pm.

After the Kids' Club Disco Dance-Off.

Before the Kids' Club Disco Dance-Off I was tense and nervous because, as you know, I'm not a very good dancer. Tennis and swimming (in pools) are my things, while dressing up and dancing are Portia's things.

But I have to say, the Dance-Off was much more fun than I had expected. I'm not saying my dancing was brilliant, but I did have a great time.

Dill and I did the macarena. We got mixed up in the middle because we were laughing so hard. Because he was watching me the whole time and copying my every move, when I messed up he did too. But we did it! We got the others up dancing too.

Portia of the Pink Hair did her full-on ballet ensemble with Rushani and Gigi, like they were in Swan Lake or something. Rushani and Gigi even wore hot-pink wigs to match Portia's swimming cap disaster.

It was good, I suppose, and the adults who came along to watch, Gran included, thought they did well.

But if you ask me, Dill and I did a much more fun dance.

None of us won a prize though. That went to some boys who dressed up in torn jeans and jackets and did a Michael Jackson moonwalk number.

Even better than the semi-enjoyable dance-off was what happened with Ash.

He came up to me after I'd finished the macarena and said the dance was great and well done for getting everyone else up to dance too. This made me smile heaps, but then he called me Portia and everything crashed and I went hot in my cheeks and said, 'Um, I'm not my sister, I'm me.'

'Er, sorry?' he said, looking confused.

I giggled nervously and said, 'I'm not Portia. I'm me, Perse.'

Ash blushed and stared at his shoes, which were brand new white sneakers. 'Sorry. I thought you were you, but you were really the other one.'

By now we were both confused and we both cracked up.

'If it's any help, Portia has pink hair, at

least for the next few days, and I have blonde hair.'

I pointed Portia out in the crowd.

She waved and didn't seem concerned that Ash was talking to me and not her. I guess that means she's really not hung up on him after all. Which means I can stop worrying. Sometimes I do that: worry over nothing. I wouldn't recommend it.

Ash laughed. 'Er, so who was I talking to at the pool yesterday? You or Portia?'

'You were talking to me first, and then I had to go to the loo and when I came back you were talking to Portia. Sorry. We kind of played a trick on you. Well, Portia did. We don't normally do that stuff. I know it's hard to tell us apart.'

'You're right about that,' Ash said, studying my face for a long time. 'I think

I've got it. Apart from you not having pink hair, you have a teardrop-shaped mole on your cheek and Portia doesn't, right?'

'Right,' I said.

'And Portia also has more freckles and her eyes aren't as green as yours.'

'I've never noticed.'

'Take it from me, it's true. Maybe you should check next time you're with your sister.'

I grinned and said, 'I will.'

Then Ash said, 'And finally, the other way to tell you two apart is that you're always writing in your notebook at a million miles an hour.'

'It's not a notebook,' I corrected him. 'It's a travel diary. Usually I use a normal diary, but because we're on holiday I'm writing a special travel diary.'

'Can I read it?' Ash asked.

'Absolutely not! It's private.'

'Okay,' he laughed.

Then, most amazingly, he asked me if I wanted to dance.

I told him I was terrible at dancing and that Portia was much better. I pointed to where she was bootscooting up a storm with Rushani and Gigi and trying to get some other boys to join them.

'If it's okay,' Ash said, 'I'd rather dance with you.'

I grinned and said, 'Sure.'

So I had my first ever real dance with a boy where I wasn't at school being forced to do it because it was raining and we couldn't do sport.

Gran even took a photo of Ash and me grooving away.

Here it is.

Check out Portia in the background with her pink hair!

Saturday 1 May. 11:11 am.
Second last day of our holiday.

We have decided to make the most of our last few days in Fiji. No more Kids' Club for us kids. No more writing for Gran. We're all hanging out by the pool sipping mocktails, sunbaking and having fun. Rushani, Gigi and their families are here, too, as well as Ash and some boys from Kids' Club.

Portia has given up her swimming cap and goggles and is swimming in the pool. She said that after the 'hot-pink hair debacle', surely nothing else could go wrong. You should have seen the way she inched into the pool, though, and it wasn't even cold!

Gran said we simply must have dinner with our new friends and their families before we go. For a change, we're going to the Japanese teppanyaki restaurant on the other side of the resort rather than the buffet.

I have no idea what teppanyaki is, but I love sushi so surely it must be good. I found out that Gigi and Rushani love sushi, too, so it seems we have finally found something in common!

Seriously, this has been the best holiday ever. I don't want to go home, although I do miss Mum.

I climbed the coconut tree a while back to check Gran's phone messages. There was a text from Mum. Apparently, she and Mr Divine are going to see a movie tonight. She seems happy, which is good.

Saturday 1 May. 9:07 pm.

Hotel bedroom. On the top bunk.

Here is a photo from our dinner at the Japanese restaurant. Who would have guessed Portia was good at catching raw eggs in a bowl: not!

We did have fun, though, and I ADORED the food. I even ate the prawn's legs. Yum!

I'm so tired. I must get some sleep in preparation for our final day in Fiji tomorrow.

Sleep tight.

Mum rang to say she would meet us at the airport, which means she has to drive through the city. She hates traffic, it freaks her out, so I'm guessing she missed us.

I wonder if Mr Divine will drive her there. After being away for two weeks, I am keen to see Mum by herself. But it doesn't bother me as much as Portia.

'I don't want to see Mr Divine,' Portia huffed. 'I hope Mum doesn't expect me to talk to him.'

That's typical Portia. She's often rude to Mr Divine. I think it's because she's secretly hoping Mum and Dad will one day get back together. She should know that's never going to happen because

Dad is with EEK now.

At the resort we said some tearful goodbyes to Rushani and Gigi, who aren't leaving until tomorrow. Of course, Ash isn't going anywhere because he lives at the resort. We all promised to write to each other. As a parting gift, I gave Rushani, Gigi and Ash a diary each, which Gran brought from the resort boutique for me.

They all promised to start their diaries straight away. I hope they keep it up. Now we have two things in common: sushi and diaries.

It's always the way, just when I get to know someone, I have to go.

Mr Divine was with Mum when she picked us up at the airport. I knew it! It seems they are closer than ever. They were holding hands and looking very happy when they met us off the plane.

Portia was fuming at first. I could tell by the set of her shoulders and the way her lips were puckered all dry and tight like she needed some lip gloss.

Portia sent me a SECRET SIGNAL that said, 'Does he have to be here?' I shook my head to tell her to calm down, and then Mum hugged us. It was a good hug too. It showed that she missed us.

After that, Portia was quite happy. I think

the hug from Mum really helped. The fact that Mr Divine had our missing luggage probably helped too. Apparently, Mum had been notified that it had arrived back at the airport a few hours before she was due to pick us up. By the number of tags on our bags, it looked like they had been around the world several times before making it home. If only bags could talk, I'm sure they would have a story to tell.

Mr and Mrs Pickleton were at the airport too. They quickly whisked Dill away, but not before we all said goodbye. It was a teary goodbye from me, a surly one from Portia.

Gran right away asked whether Mum and Mr Divine had a nice time while we were gone. Mr Divine grinned and Mum giggled like she was about ten years old. I think that was a yes.

I will be quizzing Mum about everything later – as soon as I can get her to myself. Or at least to Portia and myself because I'm pretty sure Portia will have a few questions too. Plus, we have so much to tell her about our holiday. I can't wait to show her all the photos we took.

We're pulling into our street now and I'm coming to the end of another diary.

It's sad finishing this off.

The holiday is over and the new term starts tomorrow, so it's back to school.

One thing I am looking forward to is seeing Caitlin and Jolie and telling them all about our tropical trouble.

It's time for another diary too. As it's only a few short weeks until Portia's and my eleventh birthday, I'm sure my next diary will include loads of party plans as well as some gossip on Mum's and Mr Divine's relationship. You never know what might happen next with my totally cool (and slightly zany) family, so stay tuned.

TTFN.

Aleesah

Hi, I'm Aleesah, the author of this book.

I grew up in the country and had a lot of freedom as a nine-year-old. My older brother, my cousin and I would ride our bikes and go exploring, build cubbyhouses and billycarts, and rescue injured animals and birds. When I wasn't outdoors, I was usually curled up on my bed reading. It was quite an addiction for me and I often got into trouble for 'having my nose in a book'. I loved colouring in and won loads of prizes for my efforts. Quite shockingly, I also loved school!

I wrote stacks of stories and illustrated them with crazy stick figures. Like Perse, I kept a diary. And I can always remember desperately wishing I had an identical twin.

Serena

Hi, I'm Serena, the illustrator of this book.

I don't really look this freaky, but as an artist, I can make myself look as kooky as I like, and you need to be able to laugh at yourself sometimes.

I grew up in Melbourne with an older brother who taught me how to wrestle, an older sister who always had the coolest clothes and jewellery and a younger sister who enjoyed following me around everywhere!

I loved drawing, writing notes in my diary, dressing up our pet cat in dolls' clothes and creating mini adventures in our huge back yard. When I was nine years old, long socks were really cool, funny dresses with lots of frills and buttons were cool, straight hair was cool and even big teeth were cool... unfortunately I was not cool.

Other titles in the Totally Twins series.

www.totallytwins.com.au